D0235997

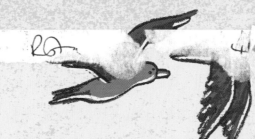

For the Neatheys
and their families.

First published in Great Britain in 2013 by Andersen Press Ltd.,
20 Vauxhall Bridge Road, London SW1V 2SA.
Published in Australia by Random House Australia Pty.,
Level 3, 100 Pacific Highway, North Sydney, NSW 2060.
Text and illustrations copyright © Richard Byrne, 2013
The rights of Richard Byrne to be identified as the author and illustrator
of this work have been asserted by him in accordance with the Copyright,
Designs and Patents Act, 1988.
All rights reserved.
Printed and bound in Malaysia by Tien Wah Press.
To create the artwork for this book Richard Byrne has hand drawn in pencil, scanned as black
and white and then coloured and composed the illustrations
using a digital drawing application.

10   9   8   7   6   5   4   3   2   1

British Library Cataloguing in Publication Data available.

ISBN 978 1 84939 568 7 (paperback)
ISBN 978 1 84939 513 7 (hardback)

This book has been printed on acid-free paper

Penguins CAN'T fly!

Richard Byrne

ANDERSEN PRESS

Once upon a time there were two eggs...

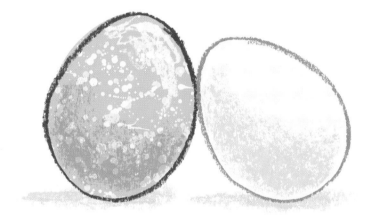

...which hatched into two little birds.
One was a gull called Gregory...

and the other was a
penguin called Hudson.

Gregory and Hudson were the best of friends.

They did everything together.

As time went on they started to grow and change,

but they remained
the best of friends.

One day, Gregory spotted a few young gulls having fun flying over the beach.

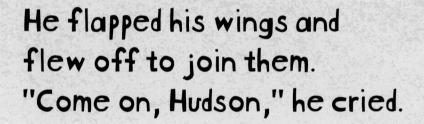

He flapped his wings and flew off to join them. "Come on, Hudson," he cried.

Hudson flapped and flapped
his little wings and...

"**W**hat use is a bird that can't fly?"
jeered Gregory's new friends.

"**I CAN fly!**" said Hudson crossly.

"I'll show them!" he thought.

But no matter
how hard he tried,

"Maybe I can't fly after all,"
sniffed Hudson to himself.
"I am useless."

Meanwhile the gulls were busy
showing off to each other.

"Watch me dive!" squealed Gregory.

Hudson and the gulls waited for Gregory to return to the surface...

...and they waited... and they waited... until...

...Hudson, sensing something was wrong, dived into the water and swam down to the sea bed.

Gregory was tangled in a fisherman's discarded net!

Hudson brought Gregory to the surface and pulled him safely onto a rock.

Gregory couldn't thank
Hudson enough.

The other gulls felt ashamed and agreed
that even though Hudson couldn't fly,
he was a great friend...

...and a brilliant diver...

...especially when it came to catching supper!